...AND
THEN
THERE
WERE
NONE

Please view my Amazon Author Page:

http://www.amazon.com/-/e/B00IQD7OMA

Get this book *free* of charge by signing up on my website, http://pro-wordsmith.net.

...AND THEN THERE WERE NONE

M. Carling

Copyright

Other Books by this author

TO THE READER: M. Carling is my alter ego
assumed for the following books of fiction.

Time Travel
And Then There Were None
Windswept Dunes – The Burning Heart-Vol. 3
Windswept Dunes – The Singing Sands (upcoming
2016)-Vol. 1
Windswept Dunes – Chameleon (upcoming
2016)- Vol. 2

I

Time Travel

The silence was palpable. Deep, deafening,
penetrating. What I had taken for granted as
background noise suddenly was missing! How odd, I
thought - I felt it in my gut. No droning air
conditioning compressors, no cars rushing by, no
generators - nothing. Just the rustling leaves of the
few trees that remained. Just the sound of the wind
as it slashed around the debris, voohooosh,
voohooowoosh - a low whistling, marauding
gangster on the prowl - whoooo, whoooo. Eerie.

Too shocked to react, not knowing how to react,
I held mute to the carnage. Strewn tree branches,

what looked like rusted cars that lay upside down, bricks and broken glass, children's toys. Chaos. I walked aimlessly amid the wreckage, without energy, without a goal. Drained of spirit, unable to make sense of what had happened. Where was everyone? There was no one, and nothing was recognizable. Even the ubiquitous chirping of birds was absent. Nothing.

As if the wind had been given free rein to howl and cause havoc, it kept up its tirade, blocking out my thoughts, my very soul.

And then I heard it. A tiny sound. A sigh, maybe? Perhaps, but it was just the wind bending a branch or chafing against something, a restless wind blowing unfettered through the mayhem. No! It is not the wind! I heard it again! A hushed sigh, muffled, faint, passing softly across the void ... unlike the howling wind. Again ... a faint, strange, muffled sound. A far-off sigh mingled with the sighing wind across the branches ... My sinew awoke, and I strained to listen, cocking my head to absorb its direction. Where was it? What was it – there, again! Faint, too faint, weak ... Where are you?! I quickened my steps, stumbling over rocks and branches, moving raggedly toward the hush.

That sound was haunting me. The wind kept howling as if hell bent on confusion. With a mind of its own, it seemed to wish to confabulate, obfuscate. Was I dreaming?

That I had been rendered alone in the world did not occur to me. It had not even entered my consciousness at that point. Humans did not simply appear on earth – they evolved. And they evolved in groups. My mind would not even entertain the concept of complete solitude.

So where was everyone??

That sigh again ...

I AM NOT IMAGINING THINGS!!! There it is again! Over there ...

I focused my attention as I strained to hear, to separate the hissing from that other sound. I cocked my head, my ear to the ground – the confusion, the crunch of leaves underfoot, and that damn wind! Shh, where is that sigh ... who is there? WHO'S THERE?

There it is again ... I can hear – it is not a sigh, it is a moan, a cry of pain ...

3

Then I saw it. A bare foot beneath a thick branch that had broken off in the melee. I dared not touch it, as if touching the dead would somehow confer death upon me. But curiosity always won in these cases. I poked at the heel with a stick I found nearby. I was not quite sure what I expected the foot to do! I poked it again. Nothing. I immediately mobilized my entire being, shoving branches aside, bare hands shoveling dead leaves as if somehow I could resurrect a dead foot. Who was this? Man or woman did not matter - it was human! I dove into the task, huge gestures, pushing, pulling, scraping damp rotten leaves away, rushing toward the face. His muddy cheeks, his lips purple-blue, hair a dirty blond, matted and snarled, his complexion sallow and dry ... but he was alive! His eyes fluttered as they tried to open, and his chest heaved.

He was moaning in pain. I touched his shoulder, then moved him more vigorously. He would not arouse. "Hey, sir! Sir? Where are you hurt?" But he only moaned. He lay on his side, his left arm awkwardly bent beneath his body, his legs pulled up to his chest, his face in the mud. As he struggled to breathe, a leaf fluttered near his nostril. I cleared the area around his face, and attempted to turn his head, but found the entire enterprise far too difficult. I had to do something - I could not let him

4

struggle for breath, or worse ... Gathering whatever strength I had, I pulled his legs straight, then somehow managed to loosen his left arm and free it from beneath his body. He seemed to breathe relief as I did so, as if an enormous strain had been lifted. Now he lay slightly askew, still on his side but much freer. He was young. I would not contemplate his age. I wanted to arouse him, to find his injury and help him. Then I saw it ...

It was dark and murky, almost sudsy in texture. Like a thick cloud of dust hovering over a night scene, the remnants of a sand storm. Mysterious and ... would I call it malevolent? The pit of my stomach tightened and my breathing hung in suspense, like a tiger at the ready. Hunched back, eyes wide, I could not name it. I could not see it. It was a feeling, a sinister, crawling sensation, a sense of impending danger. What was it!?

It hung in midair, a mass of ugly stench, at times changing colors from a blackish gray to putrid green. Sharp flashes of lightning streaked across the mass, crackling loudly, the only sound besides the deafening wind.

And the moans from my injured companion.

The day was passing fast into dusk, that time where nothing is clearly outlined. The dread I felt was now compounded by worry, nay, downright fright. What had been chaotic, unexplainable, unfathomable would become downright treacherous under the darkness of night.

What was that horrid cloud hovering over the devastation?

I felt too confused to think. The total destruction of the life I had known, my sudden aloneness, this poor injured chap ... and that ominous cloud. To make some sense of it all would require the mind of a giant, and at the moment I could not feel any more childlike and vulnerable!

A cry of pain jolted me from whatever reverie I might have entertained, and rallied me to action. I bent to the young man, looked around frantically to find some help, then stood and called out. If others were within ear shot, I hoped they would come to our aid. But my calls went unanswered. Indeed, my shouts were drowned by the eerie sound of the malevolent wind and the fiery crackles from that odd cloud. I could not be heard by anyone.

Despair began to court me. Helplessness and a sense of nakedness and impotence prevailed. What could I do to help that young man?

He cried in pain as I bent over him. The day was getting darker, and his injuries would be increasingly difficult to attend to without benefit of light. If I were to help him, I had to get to work.

"Tell me what hurts ... can you hear me? What's your name?" I felt desperate to help, to save him from his misery before nightfall. At first he only moaned in pain. I frantically pushed him for some words, anything to help me know how to proceed. "What's your name?" It then occurred to me that badgering him would not help. I ran my hands rapidly over his body, looking for what, I was not sure ... perhaps as a way to locate the source of his pain. As I got to his right leg, I heard his muffled voice. "Mark. My name is Mark."

I hurried to look at him. "Mark! Can you tell me what hurts? I want to help. I think we're all alone here!"

It seemed like the only way to make contact with him, and yet just knowing he was alive was enough. He writhed and winced in pain, and I realized he no doubt hurt all over and would not be

7

able to engage in meaningful conversation. I was on my own.

I used the hem of my blouse to wipe his face, and stroked his hair back. He closed his eyes for a moment, then opened them wide again. "It came from nowhere ... I don't know ... where ..." Then he closed his eyes again, and seemed to lose consciousness.

I knew it was pointless to try to arouse him again, yet staying where we were, among the rubble, without shelter was frightening. Still, I had very little choice at the moment.

Dusk was coming fast. It wrapped us in a blanket of misty fog of unclear edges. Beyond, the malevolent-looking cloud flashed threatening strikes of light.

I lay next to him, hoping that my body would warm him a bit. I had found him buried in mud and rubble, certainly not a comfortable spot to spend the night. As frightened as I felt, I was also glad not to be totally alone. Yet an injured companion was hardly very reassuring.

We slept together. Somehow the wailing wind soothed our frazzled nerves. Mark was mostly unconscious through his pain, and I had become resigned to our helplessness. The ground and caked mud were cold. Ordinarily, I could not sleep in these circumstances, but shock and fatigue took over, and allowed me some needed rest.

Throughout the night, Mark moaned and writhed. He clutched to me, and I to him, hoping that our body heat would keep us alive.

And the wind kept up its chant, a constant menace amid the rocks and debris.

When I opened my eyes again, it was light. A strange hue permeated the atmosphere. A kind of yellowish-bluish tinge hung in the air. I then remembered the disaster of the previous day and panicked. *What happened,* I wondered out loud. *Where is everyone?* I felt a tugging at my sleeve, and remembered. Mark was awake, looking a bit better than the previous day, disheveled and pale, but awake.

He attempted a very weak smile. His cracked lips would not permit more. "You're up!" I cried out in excitement. "How're you feeling?" But he did not answer, and I realized that he probably could not speak. I also became painfully aware of my own hunger and thirst, and other biological needs.

9

Everything had been held in suspense while in crisis mode; but after a night's rest, bodily functions began to come to the fore. My sense of modesty was still in high gear, despite the conditions we were experiencing. I began to look around frantically for a spot of privacy, but everywhere was devastation. As my needs became more urgent, I began to walk amid the broken concrete shards, looking back periodically to orient myself within the rubble so as to find my way back. It would be unthinkable to separate from the only other person alive in this wasteland. But was he? I did not know and at that moment would not even contemplate such possibility.

I found what looked like the remnants of a wall still standing. It would have to serve as privacy shelter. But would I be visible to others on the other side, I wondered. In a moment of sheer desperation, I squatted down and relieved myself. If anyone was watching, I thought rebelliously, *have a good look, 'cuz you probably ain't never seen this before!* But there came no lewd cackling or jeering; no base construction guys peering from scaffolding; no truckers posturing with their peers. There was no one around! Nothing, except for that infernal wailing wind that was beginning to get on my nerves.

There was also no toilet paper, or even water.
My scrupulous habits were being sorely challenged.
I wondered absently how the primitives remained
free of disease? Or even the people who lived during
the Middle Ages! What was I going to do? How was
I going to keep clean?

Never mind cleanliness, I was hungry and
thirsty. Was there any water or food anywhere? I got
up, and began to contemplate my next challenge.
Even my very humble beginnings sixty seven years
earlier had not prepared me for life in the wild. But
this was not the wilderness. The trees were devoid of
the screams of monkeys in the canopy. Where were
the birds? This was not the wilderness of the movies;
it was a cityscape. Devastated to be sure, but city
nevertheless! Broken glass and tortuous metal
pilings – not forests and limpid pools.

My reverie carried me to *Cast Away* where the
character of Tom Hanks is marooned on a desert
island, and through sheer intelligence and
determination, he manages to survive by putting to
use his imagination in taming the wild. One of my
favorite movies, rich in invoking one's native ability
to survive. But this was different. There was
absolutely nothing familiar here. If I was to devise a

way to survive, I would need a frame of reference, something to anchor my imagination.

Suddenly, I heard a call. I rushed toward the spot where I had left Mark.

It was a faint cry, muffled by the crackling and flashing lights from the cloud. I was not sure it was Mark, but then, I had seen no one else. And a sound that was human in this strange place was cause for increased attention.

When I arrived, Mark was not there. What ... where had he gone? He did not seem to be in any condition to walk around! Besides, I was gone no more than 5 minutes! Oh, please, no! I cannot be alone, not here! My only companion ...

But he soon reappeared, limping badly, his shirt torn, his slacks mere shreds on his legs.

"Where did you go?!"

"You were gone for such a long time, I went to find you. I can't see anyone else around! What's going on?"

I had no answers. Worse, time did not seem to fit what I had remembered. I thought I was merely gone a few minutes, while he had the impression that I was absent much longer. This was very unsettling.

"Where are we?" he asked, "and what the heck happened here?"

I could not tell him, so I tried my hand at a bit of levity: "We're in a parallel world. We're gonna find some green-haired creatures coming out of the woodwork at any moment!"

He was not amused. Frankly, neither was I.

WHERE THE HELL WERE WE? WHAT HAD HAPPENED TO THE WORLD I KNEW?

The ominous cloud continued to strike lightning. Oddly, it did not change shapes, did not dissipate, did not expand – it just hung in midair, enormous, threatening, dark.

I would not relinquish the bit of humor I felt. The emotions I felt were ... what were they? Confused! I did not know whether to laugh or cry. I was hungry, dirty, and had an injured companion with no ability to care for him. The night was cold, and we had no shelter. I did not even know if we were still in the same town, much less the same world!

But such thoughts were absurd. It must have been some natural disaster that leveled our city, cut out all electricity, which in turn impeded water flow.

But what of the people?? Where was everyone? This seemed unfathomable! Cars were strewn everywhere, some upside down, willy-nilly on what was left of streets, between concrete pilings ... it was chaos.

Mark hopped onto his good leg and plopped down on a piece of concrete beside me, and began to gingerly and delicately peel away the fabric of his slacks, revealing a nasty gash on his lower leg. The bone was protruding, jagged and raw. He winced in pain. I knelt at his feet to get a better look. "Mark, I'll have to do something for your wound. I'm not quite sure ... I have nothing ... wait. Tear off one of the sleeves from your shirt. I'll go find a stick."

Whatever first aid I had been taught now began to make sense. I combed the debris, and located a suitable branch, and used a stone to strip it as best I could of leaves and bark, creating a clean splint. I rushed back to Mark. "Mark, I will have to push the

14

bone back into your leg. You can't let it heal this way. It's going to hurt like hell." Ordinarily rather squeamish, I gathered all my fortitude, palpated his lower leg for best positioning of the broken bone, then in a swift push-pull action, set the bone back next to its broken fragment.

Poor Mark. I could not save him from this pain. He screamed and grasped my shoulder and squeezed it painfully. He held onto it until the pain became familiar and somewhat acceptable. I tried to squirm away from his tight grasp, but found myself yielding into it. I hastened to wrap his leg in the sleeve from his shirt, then caressed his face that was twisted in agony.

I marveled at my own courage. Even in ministering care, one had to remain detached enough in order to inflict this kind of pain on another.

In short course, Mark regained his composure. "I'm hungry" he said. Hungry?? Are you kidding? You've got a wound the size of Nebraska and you think of food!?

Yes, well, I was hungry, too. It had been a long time since I had eaten last, and to hear Mark tell it, my sense of time was questionable!

15

What. Was. Going. On??? Where were we? What was that infernal cloud that was not moving from its stationary spot in midair? And where was everybody??

I mused with the silly notion that we had been taken by some extraterrestrials to another planet. I certainly had seen enough movies! But why would they destroy all the other humans, if in fact they were destroyed? More to the point, why did they keep us alive? Or had we been the only ones abducted? And what of the animals?

Odd questions. I could not make sense of what was happening. I toyed with that thought again, wondering why a culture from another world would wish to create a parallel world to ours; or to destroy all that was here on earth - if we were still on earth - or to keep alive two such disparate people! Did they expect us to mate and start a new race? At sixty-seven, my childbearing years were over! Mark, on the other hand, was young and virile, but that would not do us any good. Besides, this was not the Bible – two are not really enough to produce a new race without risking serious mutations. No, that made no sense.

My mouth felt terribly dry. Parched. My lips were chapped and cut and had begun to bleed. I had no energy or voice to cry out. I looked at Mark, and he hardly was in better shape. We would have to find food and water, or we would perish.

Again I thought about the poor planning of those extraterrestrials. If they thought we would create a new race, they should have planned for food and water!

I was becoming giddy.

The day fell into night once more. The watch on my arm had stopped working. We had not eaten nor found water, but the ragged edges of shock were beginning to smooth over, if ever so slightly. We could not make sense of things, and were rapidly dissolving into unconsciousness. If we were to survive, we would have to find a source of sustenance. Things looked very grim.

Before daylight had ebbed entirely, we halfheartedly gathered some sticks of wood, placed them in a mound, and got down to the task of rubbing two stones together. The stones got hot in our hands before the fire was lit, but eventually, with sheer perseverance, we managed to light it. We had both rubbed those stones feverishly, and when the first sparks flew out and landed on the kindling, we burst out shouting joyously.

17

Such simple triumphs spurred us on at a time of sheer bleakness.

We huddled together on the ground, sheltered by a wall remnant from a fallen building. The ground felt cold, colder than the ambient air. We held each other tightly in an attempt to create some body heat. The fire crackled gently, yet did not become a raging pyre. Our survivalist skills would have to be sharpened.

Would we survive the night?

Mark was shivering. I held him tightly. The softness of my body should be of some comfort to this slender young man. He held me tightly, then seemed to relax in my arms, and I heard the regular deep breaths of the sleeping soul.

In time, I too slept.

I awoke in a start. It seemed to be early still, the faintest rays of light streaking behind that ominous stationary cloud. I could see the vague outline of my companion. Mark was snoring softly, his head buried in the crook of his arm. I wondered how he could sleep so profoundly with so much pain, not to mention the deepening hunger.

My lips felt incredibly dry, so much so that I could barely open my mouth. I began to wonder how much longer we could go on this way. I determined to start looking for sources of food or water as soon as Mark awoke. We had to do something ...

Our dire predicament served as backdrop to vague memories of my life before this – what was it, exactly? I could not say. I recalled my upcoming appointment with my attorney, and the meeting with my publisher that I had missed. Damn! I had spent many sleepless nights attempting to get an audience with him. What an ironic turn of events!

"Hi," I heard Mark stir behind me. "I slept pretty deeply."

Deeply, I mused. The kid's educated!

"What's your name, if you don't mind my asking?"

Oh, I love this – he's educated *and* polite! And I have to be marooned on this ... whatever this is, to meet such a nice young man!

The operative word here was *young!* How ironic. Mark could not be older than 30! And he was

19

handsome. A bit pale for my tastes, but handsome. How was it possible that I was entertaining thoughts of beauty in the midst of hunger and disorientation and shock?

Such musings scoured my consciousness. "Please tell me your name ... we may as well get to know each other."

"Oh, sorry, I'm Elyse."

"Elyse? Just Elyse?"

"Elyse Prescott. I was born Elyse MOnvalet, but kept my second husband's name. It seemed easier to pronounce."

"Ah, you're married, then ..."

"Divorced. But frankly, out here, it doesn't much matter, does it?"

How could we talk with such a dry mouth? I felt beyond desperate for water. The thirst was so intense, my throat tightened with every breath. Yet here we were, carrying on a conversation!

"Mark, we must search for food and water. I have no idea where to begin, but we can't stay here and wait."

We stood and began to walk aimlessly in a direction we did not know. We instinctively looked on the path at our feet, at the upturned rocks, the loose sand, the glass debris. We searched as if looking for dropped coins! There was nothing that remotely resembled anything edible. No pools of standing water, no fruit, not even insects. What a strange place! Not even lizards baking in the sun!

I suddenly realized something: The sun was rising in the horizon, just as I had remembered, and had done so the prior two days! That was encouraging. The temperature, too, was rising. Except for that horrid, ugly, immovable cloud, the weather, at least, was what I remembered.

But why such devastation? I could not remember what happened. Could not recall a weather event of such magnitude as to destroy a city; did not recall terrorist attacks; could not recall a war ... nothing to explain the current landscape. Not to mention the lack of any life save the two of us!

In my daydreaming, I had not noticed that Mark and I had become separated.

"Elyse! Elyse!"

I turned to see Mark crouched down a few meters behind me, with a huge grin on his face. How energizing it was to find something unexpected in a desolate place, even for one who had been so badly injured!

I rushed to him, stepping over stones and broken branches. Mark had the biggest smile on his face as he pointed to the ground. There was a leaf, green and plump, cradling a tiny drop of water.

Buoyed by the discovery of even such a small speck of hope, we rallied in our search. I hopped and ran and skipped over debris, Mark in toe limping badly but doing his best to mimic my jubilant dance, both looking for the source of that drop of water – anything to quench our thirst; anything at all that would reassure us that life would remain.

We found none.

Was this a mirage? The psychological torment of the subconscious that produced hallucinations?

Nearly simultaneously, we dissolved in laughter. Riotous, belly-tightening laughter. "Mark, we're doomed. I don't know about you, but I'm beginning to wonder if we're on another planet." Mark merely smiled.

Another day had passed. We had surrendered to discharging our bodily functions in whatever privacy we could devise, even as those functions were dwindling fast. The light was dimming again, and we began to search for a suitable place to lay our tired bodies for another night that may be our last.

Mark lay his head on his bent arm and almost immediately fell asleep. It was barely dark. I remained sitting, hugging my knees, thinking. Wondering how we would survive. *If* we would survive. At this rate, we would need divine intervention if we were to stay alive. We both were intelligent, yet no amount of creativity or resourcefulness would reveal anything that would keep us alive. Sometimes surrender tends to open the imagination more than the stress of being in survival mode.

Sometimes.

Meanwhile, I was hungry. I was surprised that my body had not relinquished my appetite. Surely it would abate soon ...

My reverie was interrupted by a sensation of something touching my hip. I let out a yelp in surprise. Even though the past three days had not revealed any other living creature, habits die hard.

"Elyse, it's only me." If I worried that anything was crawling on me, I certainly did not expect this. He tugged at my clothing, "Come here. Lie with me."

Lie with me? Was he merely cold? I recalled our previous night when we huddled together for warmth, and I lay next to him. He put his arm around me and nuzzled me. "I'm so glad you were here to fix my leg. I have no idea what's going on, but it's good to have someone here."

"Yes, it is," I agreed.

He then touched my cheek, caressed it a moment, then placed his lips upon mine. Dry and chapped, but with a soft touch, a tender kiss. I did not pull away.

We slept soundly and awoke to the rising sun. I was aware that he was still holding my hand. He looked up at me with tender eyes.

"We're in a pickle, aren't we?" I smiled at the allusion.

"Yes, I'd say we are. If we don't find some basic sustenance, I'm afraid ..."

"I propose we keep searching, then." He said. "We cannot give up, Elyse! Perhaps we can devise something, though I can't imagine what ... we haven't found any source of water anywhere."

"No ... what can we do? Where do we go from here?"

Mark sat at my side, and put his arm around me. He said nothing for a while, then "Last night was wonderful. Under the circumstances ..."

"Yes. Under the circumstances, although ..." I smiled wryly.

If his kiss was awkward and dry, his hand on my breast was softness itself. Tenderness and gentleness seemed in such direct contrast to our deepening misery and despair. I yielded to his touch.

"Although what? Do you regret it?"

"No, not really, I'm merely curious how you could find me remotely attractive in the circumstances?"

"Attractive? You are downright beautiful!"

25

"Mark, I'm probably old enough to be your grandmother!"

"I don't think so, but even so, you are beautiful – and quite desirable!"

Desirable? Dirty and disheveled, my countenance pallid and drawn ... was he merely being polite? That would be rich, in this godforsaken desperate place! Yet his good manners remained. It was lovely.

Mark Winston was 36, the son of a rich industrialist, on his way to Paris when all he knew seemed to disappear. During our search for food and water the previous day, he talked about his life. His sister had been working in Africa with Doctors Without Borders, and had taken a sojourn in Paris, and he was off to see her. They were very close, spending their childhood and later life connected as bolster against their busy and detached parents. He had learned the rules of etiquette that permitted him to hobnob with his father's colleagues and clients, and had the necessary acumen to study international finance abroad and join his father's company. He had risen through the ranks as much for his brilliant negotiating skills as for his good looks. He made his father proud.

Now this. Whatever "this" was.

The night had been as deafeningly quiet as the day. Nothing resembled my former life. No siren sounds, cars speeding, the ubiquitous televisions, people talking on their phones. Except for my companion, there was nothing. The eerie absence of any sound at all was disconcerting and unsettling.

Even sleep was odd in the dead silence. I had learned to absorb a lot of background noise in my former existence.

The night when Mark touched me was no different. Dead silence, profound, down to my bones, a sort of vacuum in my brain. He lay next to me, then touched my breast, and I shivered. I said nothing as he came closer and kissed the crook of my neck. How was it possible that in these awful conditions, I could still feel aroused? Indeed, how was it possible that through my hunger and fatigue, I could still respond?

I marveled at the magnificence of the human body. At my age, bone tired and with no small measure of angst and fear, I felt the rising warmth in my loins, just as Mark had begun to breathe more deeply and insistently. He held me close and stroked his stubbly chin against my cheek. Where that might have ordinarily discouraged any further response, in our current state, it was erotic. I felt warm as his manhood pressed against me, and I sighed into his embrace. We undulated on the hard ground amid the bricks and rubble until the moment when all seemed to fade away in a lurch of emotion that carried us both heavenward.

The only sound to break the silence was our throaty cries.

Our strange existence continued unabated. Thirst and hunger settled into the background as a gnawing ache, and fatigue gave way to a sort of resignation. We seemed to reach a level of acceptance of our strange new milieu. Panic and angst were replaced by surrender to the elements, such as they were: a dread quiet save for the roar of the wind and our own hoarse voices. We spent more time in mute reflection, perhaps as a way to encourage our own demise. We didn't dare wonder how either of us would survive if left alone by the death of the other. Survive? This wasn't living ...

Periodically, one of us would utter a few words of mirth, as if comic relief could soften the raw edges of our situation. In a way, it did just that. What else was there? We had become so accustomed to our technologically advanced lives with our

28

comforts and the people who moved in and out of our existence! Were we being tested? Was this some sort of philosophical exercise?

"Boy, I can only imagine how panicky my mother must be not to be able to reach me!"

"Where's your mom?" Mark seemed like a lovely young man, someone I might have liked to know in another life.

"My mother is currently in a nursing home," I said. "She's not a very easy patient – not a very easy person. I'm feeling guilty in her regard, even though I know I shouldn't, and now this! She must be out of her mind."

I must have appeared anxious as I said this, because he didn't respond, but just put his arm around my shoulder. "Not much you can do about it now, is there?"

No, there was not. Ironically, I felt relieved. The situation we were in was not of my making, yet it freed me from the crushing responsibility I had taken on to nurture and coddle my mother. She had been cantankerous and onerous, frequently demanding and unstable, yet through it all, I had remained faithful and loyal to her, even though I had often entertained thoughts of simply disappearing. How ironic, I had now done just that – through no planning of my own!

Or did I? Where was personal responsibility? Did I not hold to the belief that we are all ultimately entirely responsible for our lot in life – the good and the bad in it? How could I now hide behind this perceived occurrence that seemed like something from a Sci-Fi book?

"Elyse, where have you gone? You seem so far away …" I had evidently begun to daydream about my life in the other realm, the one I used to know, the one I now missed. My friends, my work, my favorite programs – all had now vanished in this surreal existence. I could no more make sense of my current circumstances as to talk about it. Neither one of us had any frame of reference. We both still experienced our biological needs, yet even those seemed somehow foreign and detached. Our need for privacy gave way to insouciance as our deepening hunger and thirst assumed a place in the background. The only thing familiar was the ebb and flow of each day, the rising daylight and the dark of night.

We both were startled out of our reverie by a crushingly loud flash from the perpetual cloud. I let out a yell and instinctively clutched Mark. He was none the calmer. "What the hell was that?!"

"If we don't see another human soon, ... "

Another streak of blinding light crashed from the cloud. The flashing had been a fairly constant phenomenon until now, blending into our strange background, rattling off in the distance, but now the cloud seemed deliberately hostile. It was as if we had somehow offended it and it was scolding us.

"Mark, I know this is all a dream. I know we will both wake up in our respective beds and chalk it all up to some mirage ... I can't imagine any other scenario, can you?"

"I don't like this any more than you do, Elyse. If I wake up in my own bed in my apartment in New York, I'll be glad I had met you, Elyse. Even if only in my dreams."

Another flash from the purple cloud, this time with sparks that scintillated very close to our feet.

"Much as I miss my life, if this is a dream from which I'll awaken, I'll relish my memory of you, Mark. That you could find me attractive in this desolate situation will carry me for a long time ..."

31

I was gazing at the cloud, bracing myself for another flash when Mark came up behind me that put his arms around me in a deep hug. It was erotic feeling his growing manhood against me and I sighed. He turned me to face him and gazed deeply into my eyes. He was as disheveled as I felt I was, yet his eyes were moist and loving. They penetrated me deeply. He said nothing as he peeled away my tattered clothes. I stood before him in my nakedness, still a bit bashful, but his admiration soon cloaked my sensibilities in eroticism and I yielded to his touch. His right hand reached down as his left hand clasped my waist, and he guided me gently as we both lay down. He persisted, moving from the softness between my legs to the gentlest feathering of his fingers on my belly and breasts. With his parched lips he tickled my nipples just as his beardly stubble stroked my skin. Where was all this passion coming from? I felt wet and hot, tingly and hungry for him until he finally plunged into me with a throaty groan. If this was a dream, I never wanted to awaken from it.

We lay together, holding each other close, as the cloud continued its dissonant fireworks and the relentless wind scattered debris.

Life on the edge continued unabated. We had almost given up searching for food. There were no living things that we could discern other than the trees and ourselves. We climbed them periodically, searching for something, anything that would reassure us that things were normal, but found none – no caterpillars, no snakes, no buzzing insects. How did these trees remain alive? With no pollination, it seemed impossible.

But everything about this place seemed impossible. Not the least of which was the fact we were still alive! Mark's injury seemed to heal, and our hunger and thirst blended into the background. Best of all, our lovemaking was wonderful, far more than I would have imagined in my former life. The stress of daily living, my mother, my son, my husband – all disappeared into a vague memory replaced by this strange reality. I had stopped wondering what cataclysmic event had brought us here, or why were we the only two. At that moment, I wanted so much to pick up the phone and call my son, only to become crushingly aware of the futility of that desire, when I heard Mark cry out.

Instinctively, my heart stopped and I froze, my senses heightened, my hearing piqued to identify the direction of his voice, my eyes widened as I searched for my companion.

"Mark! Mark!! Where are you?! Mark ..."

I panicked when I got no reply. We had gotten used to staying close by. "MARK! Please, where are you?!"

I ran, tripping over debris and loose stones, frantically searching in every direction for my one source of solace.

II

...and Then There Were None

I found him standing before a broken pillar at the side of an enormous expanse of steps which led to what looked like a substantial edifice of some kind. I followed Mark's gaze toward a retaining wall with the inscription 3284. Was that an address? Mark suddenly seemed to spot something further away, and ran toward it. It was a fragment of a sign with the letters *EUM* inscribed upon it. 3284. *EUM.*

We scoured the rubble for anything else that might be recognizable. There were shards of pottery and tattered paintings, some of familiar animals. We climbed the steps and stood on what was a stunningly beautiful circular hall, with a marble floor and the remnants of marble columns. The wind had wreaked havoc there, too, but we could find objects that had meaning to us. One exhibit portrayed lions, with various inscriptions describing them as having lost their habitat. Further on, we discovered a broken display of a stuffed lion with the inscription, "*The last of its kind.*"

Similar displays and inscriptions were scattered everywhere. Familiar animals, elephants, snakes, even the butterflies and inspects carried captions of their disappearance. Everywhere we looked were vestiges of a vanishing species.

What kind of place was this?

"Dogs were once considered man's best friend, now man himself is gone."

III

There was a time when the Arabian sheiks
controlled the flow of oil, taking in vast fortunes
while rival nations vied for equal prominence.
Geography had generously graced the entire region
with the fossil remains of prehistory. Those peoples
that lived on the edge of the sand were able to dig
into the belly of the earth and extract the oil. This in
turn oiled machinery that would become a powder
keg in the politics of the region with virulent
tentacles spreading worldwide. A despot in old
Mesopotamia set a neighboring country's oil fields
afire as a way to prevent any other country from
taking control. That it backfired against the tyrant
was seemingly lost on the world, and clashes over oil
persisted unabated.

But oil would see its glory go the way of the dinosaurs. The Americas developed technology that dredged oil from its gut, thus moving away from its reliance on the Middle East. With plentiful oil, the car manufacturers rolled in money as more and more people purchased huge trucks, small compacts, vans and buses that choked the highways as their fumes choked the air. Asthma became epidemic; more serious diseases increased in incidence, diseases such as lung cancer and heart disease. But as disease became more rampant, technological advances mushroomed to the point where even cancer was no more troublesome than the common cold. People still underwent treatment, but complete cure was almost guaranteed. Of course, such facile medicine featured prominently and glibly in the marketing ploys of auto manufacturers and industry of every ilk. No commerce would yield to environmental judiciousness if its bottom line was challenged.

Indeed, the environmentalists became a thorn in industry's side, forever admonishing against growth, research or expansion, seemingly thwarting industry's objectives to increase profits by decreasing costs, sometimes at any cost, the environment be dammed.

These two factions clashed frequently, sometimes in small contained squabbles, other times in more serious debacles. Lawyers became involved as lawsuits were filed and dragged through the halls of justice, permitting them to rake in millions of dollars as they drummed up spurious technicalities and rattled off arguments meant only to obfuscate. Appeals demanded briefs, discovery, increased personnel, and the process would go on ad infinitum, until the public lost interest or the company itself lost its fortunes and was delisted from trading on the Street.

But the skirmishes over oil paled in comparison to the wars of religion. For a time, it seemed a certain group was fated to win over the entire world to its ideology if only by dint of massacres and depravity ironically reminiscent of the Crusades of the Middle Ages. But that, too, did not last. Eventually, other entities overpowered the less well-organized groups and took control, letting its citizens enjoy a few years of peace.

Technological advances were most evident in increased longevity. Within two or three generations, the average lifespan had increased from about 65 years to over 110 – and much older a few generations hence. World populations now had a wider ratio of elderly to younger people. A television magazine casually described the world population as having doubled over the prior forty years, but reassured viewers that because of declining birth rates, was anticipated to double again in two hundred years. No one felt any urgency from such news, as it would not be within one's own lifetime. Declining birth rates, however, were no match for the ever-increasing lifespans that resulted from advances in medical discoveries or their practitioners who seemed hell bent on keeping people alive by any means possible. Many dread diseases had been conquered, and drugs were now cheap and easily available to relieve pain or otherwise improve lives.

But as some illnesses disappeared, others took hold, more virulent and tenacious. Some obscure and mysterious, defying diagnosis or treatment; diseases born of chemical pollution and engineered foodstuffs; diseases that cropped up insidiously, stymying all efforts at eradication.

In time, technology could not keep up with the chronic ailments that had taken hold. Where illnesses caused by living organisms had been reduced to mere annoyances, chemically-caused diseases were on the rise. Coal had long been abolished as a source of fuel, but pollution was rampant in many other forms, sickening everything it touched, from the water to the food.

Commercially made oil and cement seemed ubiquitous in the new cities that were built at a frantic pace to accommodate the increasing masses. Yet the overwhelming mood of the people was one of insouciance, with films of happy couples skiing in fresh powder or vacationing families wading in the oceans.

It was a ploy concocted by world governments to control social unrest.

The reality was far different.

The masses were led to believe that the plains were open wide, when in fact, free land was at a premium. Propaganda was being piped in with films of the bison and the wolf of the sacred national parks, but those could now be seen only in museums. Travel itself became increasingly restricted, as countries imposed stiff quotas on tourism in an effort to curtail terrorism and the spread of infectious illnesses.

Avarice ruled. One could never be too rich. Some figures touted by the media boggled the imagination. People did not always come by their wealth honestly, and the lawyers continued to line their pockets with ever more convoluted arguments in the name of zealous representation. For some, life was good.

IV

As with all excess, the river of good fortune began to run dry. It was gradual at first, unnoticed by those not intimately involved in the machinery of obfuscation. Echoes of disaster had been made clear enough for centuries, but heeded by few.

This was the world I was born to.

"Your vittles are ready," I heard the com system announce. I hastened to collect them as was required, and consumed them quickly. After pressing the button I was provided with water. The screens on the walls lit up, and news from various corners of our world began to filter in, most of them good, with images of happy people engaged in pleasant activities.

"Your bath is ready" was the next drone from the system. As was mandated, I acquiesced. Everything about life was set to a schedule; everything was automated and required as little effort on our part as possible.

"Elyse? Where have you gone …" I heard Mark's voice pierce through my reverie.

"I was reminiscing about my life … I mean …"

"Yes, I know. What used to be our lives. What we knew, the people we knew. Now this."

We sat close to each other on a rock, looking off into the distance. Devastation was everywhere. We had not had food or water for four days, and knew our demise was imminent. We dared not speak of it.

The only sound came from the whistling wind kicking up debris as it flew by unfettered.

Mark broke the eerie silence. "Elyse, …" I suddenly fell into his arms, sobbing. I wondered where the tears had come from given my dehydrated state, but I yielded to the emotion. Mark held me silently, caressing my matted hair, trying to silence the racking sobs that emanated from the very depth of me.

"I'm sorry, Mark, I'm sorry. I don't know how we got here, I know we're both in pain, yet all I can think of is my poor mother."

"Your mother?"

"I had to place her in a facility for the aged. She is miserable there, and would wail at me regularly. I had tried to be helpful, and all I could do was make her miserable."

"Did you make her miserable, or was it her choice?"

Ah, the philosopher in him had made an appearance. At 36, Mark seemed mature beyond his years. I instinctively liked him. He had a way of pointing out the truth in few words.

"To see her sedated, hunched over in her chair, blankly staring into space is pitiful, Mark! I wish I could do something to remove her pain ..."

"That only shows that you are compassionate, Elyse, but old or young, ultimate responsibility rests with each one of us. No one does anything to us. We create our own reality."

"Including this – whatever this is?"

"I suppose so, Elyse, even if we don't comprehend what's going on. Still, we alone are experiencing our current reality."

We alone ... alone. There was no one else around. No birds, no animals. We alone.

The wind continued its harangue. A speck of dust flew into my eye temporarily stopping all conversation. "Look, Elyse, there is nothing more you can do. Your mother has made her own choices and has lived life as she saw fit, with good or bad results. You are doing the same, as I am. My father may be proud of me or disappointed, but in the end, it's my life to live – and so is yours. You cannot – must not – think of sacrificing yourself for another."

"It feels so cruel ..."

"You're such a softie, Elyse! Snap out of it! Besides, look around – what can you do now?"

I felt totally bewildered. Indeed, why was my memory intact? Why was I still living in my own time? What kind of calamity befell us that we would have such wreckage overnight?

Or was it overnight – I didn't know. I had no frame of reference.

The devastation around us was profound. Everywhere were broken shards and fallen buildings, surrounded by tufts of weeds. Moss had grown over the sides of broken walls. The trees were gone. We felt like the only humans on earth. Perhaps we were. We were tired and depleted of energy, and could barely hold onto each other in this desolate landscape. Whatever life we had left certainly seemed like a memory now. Regret, worry – nothing much mattered in the gathering darkness of our current existence.

"Let's go see if we can find some clues over there," I pointed to that imposing edifice we had come upon earlier. The only remnants were a superb marble floor and the broken columns that had flanked the enormous hall. Mark had found what looked like a sign with the letters E U M emblazoned upon it, and we both agreed it must have been a museum. The numbers 3284 inscribed on one of the columns were more mysterious.

We strolled along, going from pillar to pillar, trying to make sense of the shattered displays and their cryptic inscriptions. Little made sense. We could not recognize some of the creatures displayed in the exhibits, as they appeared more like the imaginings of sci-fi Hollywood moguls of old.

This strange museum and its discoveries fascinated me as much as it disturbed. I was so absorbed that I did not notice where Mark had gone, until I heard him call out, "Elyse! Elyyyyse!" I rushed to him, but he stood mutely, holding a piece of pottery or shell, I could not be certain. He then came up to me, still holding that fragment, put his other hand on my shoulder and looked into my eyes. His expression conveyed something ominous, though I was not sure.

"Elyse, it's not good. I think it's all over."

All over? What is all over? More than this wasteland? Was there even more? Please, Mark ...

"Whatever life we knew is gone, Elyse. Look ..."

He then almost reverently placed that broken fragment in my hand. What I read made my heart stop: 2800 Census: 76 billion.

How could it be? 76 billion *people*? That is impossible! 2800 Census? The *year* twenty-eight hundred?!

I felt dumbstruck with despair. I ran from one spot to the other, as if to remove that information from my consciousness. Mark remained standing in one spot, no doubt as stunned as I, with an expression I could not decipher. I was too astounded and disoriented to pay attention.

My mind scoured my memory banks. Seven six billion humans was untenable. The earth could not sustain that many people! Capacity had been extrapolated to just about twenty billion! WHAT WAS GOING ON HERE?!

The prospect of our imminent demise suddenly became much more real. If there was denial up to that point, this latest discovery would erase any hope.

"Mark, this can't be." I ran back to him. "We must figure out what happened – to our world, to us, to this place! Where are we? What the hell is going on?!"

I refused to believe that piece of broken shard with that insane bit of detail: 2800 Census? That is not possible. I lived in 2020! I have things to do! I have my friends … my work …

I was still thinking in the present tense. My world – but this now was my world, unless I was merely dreaming. Yes, that's it: It's all a dream! I know I shall wake up in my own bed with the filtering light of early morning, the curtains curled up in the breeze, the sound of the chirping morning birds piercing the silence. I would linger a bit under the sheets before arising, take a cup of hot fragrant coffee and begin to respond to mail. I would watch the news and arrange my day's schedule. I would speak to my mother, then plan a luncheon with a friend. I would ...

No, whatever was going on now was simply impossible.

We both continued exploration of our strange environment that yielded even stranger information. With his injured leg, Mark did his best to hop around the hall's debris, sometimes bending over to pick up an object, then tossing it aside. I watched him as he ambled to and fro, hopping or limping. I felt too shocked to participate in further inquiry – this milieu was giving me the creeps. Was this all a joke?

I heard Mark cry out to me, and ran toward him. Again, with an expression I could not understand, he said, "Things are going from strange to downright frightening. Here, take a look ..." He then handed me a fragment of something he had picked up inscribed with *"...nsus of 3100 ... 106 bi..."*

If I was not shocked before seeing this, I now felt totally numb. Unable to contain myself any longer, I burst into tears. "But I have a life! I have memories! What the hell is going on here? Where is my life?! Why was I brought here – and you? Where did you come from?"

I was once again the child, needy, vulnerable, fragile and quite emotional. I wanted answers. I wanted an anchor, a point of reference, something that would connect me to the world I knew, my real life.

Mark was no calmer. Whatever I felt was certainly shared by him – he was human, after all.

That thought struck me as amusing; Suppose he wasn't? Suppose he wasn't …

"Elyse, I have an idea," he said as he took my hand and led me toward the wide steps where we sat down. I felt weak and dizzy, as much for the lack of food and water as from shock. "Tell me about your life, Elyse. Share your memories with me. If this is all there is, …"

How do you reconstruct a life? Where do you begin? My memories were mere specters, floating hither and yon without anchor. There was nothing recognizable – not in the current landscape, nor curiously in my mind. I experienced specks of memories that did not seem real. They might as well have been snippets of dreams. How does one tell the tale of what happened so many years ago in a way that made sense now? We had no frame of reference.

"I don't think I can ... where do I begin??"

The only thoughts running through my mind were *don't ever let them see you cry.* How odd; Mark had just held me as I sobbed inconsolably.

Don't ever let them see you cry.

That thought darted through my mind as I tried to piece together some fragments of my life. My real life, before all this.

"I have nothing to hold onto," I began. "My work, my husband, my friends – nothing means anything anymore. What's the use of having memories if you can't connect them to anything?"

"Let them be a form of sustenance now, Elyse. There is nothing else. Just you and me in this vast wasteland. I miss my father, and can't imagine how he must feel – I mean, how he must have felt when this all happened … whatever this is."

"I didn't have a father," I said. "Well, of course, I had a father - everyone has a father, but my memories of him are vague and fleeting. EVERYTHING IS FLEETING RIGHT NOW!" I shouted, unable to contain myself. My nerves felt raw, my emotions felt raw, and I did not want to play a game of sublimation. I wanted to touch reality. I wanted to feel comfortable again, well fed and content. I ached to be in my own bed, drifting off to sleep as I planned the next day's tasks.

"Shh, shh," Mark held onto me tightly. He certainly seemed more mature than I. But maturity is merely socially appropriate behavior. What maturity was called for here? We were doomed. Any society that existed had vanished. Even the animals had disappeared. Nothing was left. Such dire circumstances should naturally lead to madness. My psychological training was rearing its head. Why would I need to keep it together given the circumstances? A colloquialism appropriate to the occasion might be suck it up! How ugly. I hated those colloquialisms, the disintegration of social graces, neglect of language. And yet …

No. There was no *and yet.* We had no hope of rescue, no source of food, no sign that anything or anyone else was still alive. We had no connection to anything remotely familiar to us.

I got up and paced aimlessly, searching, sniffing the air for something familiar, just as I remembered my cat behave when we first brought it home. It sniffed the floor, the furnishings, the plants, all the while crouched low to the ground, its tail hugging its flanks, then withdrew to some remote corner where it remained hidden for a few days until it felt reassured that all potential danger had passed. I was now that cat. Except that my surroundings would never assume a more pleasing shape or familiar scent; I could never crawl out of my hiding place to greet my new family and hope to be fed, petted and loved.

I was in the dungeons of self-pity and despair. Mark caressed my face and held me close. I could feel his breath on my neck, soft and warm. Incredibly, I also began to feel aroused. From the depths of anguish, in this abject wilderness, bereft of hope or energy, I felt aroused. But our bodies had shriveled from dehydration and desire would not bloom to its full experience, so we let the hours pass in silence.

It was a curious form of meditation. The deafening silence punctuated by the whistling wind and kicked-up debris, in the far horizon a familiar sky that pretended normalcy.

We waited.

V

I don't know how we passed the time until night. Somehow we fell asleep huddled together on whatever corner of soft earth we could find. The whistling wind chafed at our skin, rendering it brittle and painful. A flash of light and thunderclap suddenly woke us, and a driving rain began to fall like pellets on the ground. Water.

Water.

After days of abject misery, hunger, fatigue and thirst, we got more than we bargained for. Rivers of water washed over the desolate terrain. We both instinctively rushed around, looking for shelter. The thundering rain fell hard, soaking us. I felt energized, if a bit chilled. I decided to yield to the occasion and stripped off my tattered clothes. They clung to my skin obstinately, but then peeled off and allowed my naked body to relish this new sensation, a sensation I had all but given up all hope of feeling again. A flash of lightning revealed Mark standing mutely looking in my direction.

I danced in the water, rubbed my face clean of the mud, then turned my head upward and allowed the rain to pour into my mouth. Gulp by gulp, the cleansing water revived me. Gulp by gulp, my spirit renewed. Gulp by gulp ...

Another flash of lightning, followed by a thunderous crash among the clouds. I shivered as I felt Mark close to me. He put his hands on my shoulders, then slipped a hand to my waist and pulled me close. I had not had my fill of drink, but the touch of his body felt good. Reassuring and sexy.

The rain pelted our bodies in the night, and except for the flash of lightning, all was dark. In the midst of the disorienting storm, I began to wonder whether any seeds had survived the catastrophe and would sprout.

Mark released his hold as the rain began to let up a bit. He took my hand and led me to the museum steps where we sat on the cool wet marble. The earth emitted a strong odor of wetness that reminded me of childhood at my grandparents' home. Fridays were devoted to preparing for the Sabbath, hosing down the terrace which would emit the same odor or wet earth. The scent of vanilla echoed from our small kitchen where Grandma was baking a cake, and a cloud of smoke would puff up from Grandpa's cigarette and mingle to a chorus of evocative memories. I was transported once again to a place that no longer existed, but was very much alive in my soul.

"This rain feels good. Feels like I'm in heaven!" Mark sat beside me, his arm around my shoulder, his skin touching mine. I wondered what he was feeling, what memories had been aroused in him, but I was too involved in reminiscing my own.

The rain had abated, and the gray streaks of dawn began to appear on the horizon. We had remained seated on the marble slab, naked, enjoying the energizing water. The sweat had been washed away, and after several days of gloom and wretchedness, we had begun to get accustomed to our environment. It was inevitable that our instincts and desires would emerge from the ashes, if only as a means of psychic survival. I was not surprised, then, to feel mark's hand take my face and turn it to him. He looked into my eyes and tenderly kissed me.

His growing beard felt harsh yet sweet; and the emotion transported us to another place, more familiar, less bereft and empty.

The rain had cleared the dust and the air felt cool on our bodies. Mark held me close and I clung to him as if he were an anchor. Perhaps he was.

Perhaps he was.

VI

The oceans gave up their bounty first. Those too busy amassing their fortunes could not anticipate it. Captains of industry sat in their boardrooms sucking cigars and expensive brandy, oblivious to the menace just beneath the surface. Indeed, that menace was all too well reported. Scientists gave their urgent messages in cautionary speeches, reporters interviewed some of them, and museums presented stunningly beautiful films as a public service depicting the demise of the glaciers with admonitions of the vanishing polar bear.

But few paid attention. The polar bear did not figure even marginally in any calculation of daily life. What the people failed to acknowledge – and governments failed to sufficiently warn – was the chain of events that would ensue. The fate of some of the old national parks had now become ancient historical events. The extinct creatures were mere irrelevant specters in the minds of most. As long as vittles were provided on time, people paid no attention.

But vittles, too, were in danger of disappearing. Once land became so scarce as to make it impossible to grow enough to feed the masses, governments turned to the sea. The maligned shark had been decimated long ago, and with it the food it lived on multiplied out of control; the whale had long been hunted to extinction for its blubber and baleens, with the result that krill had increased to inconceivable proportions, choking the food supply of other creatures. When the oceans succumbed to the excesses of humankind, industry and government resorted to artificially produced foodstuff.

* * *

The oceans had become dark and murky, soiled with industrial debris, filthy with the carcasses of the dead and dying. It had become a receptacle for discards of every kind.

What could not be burned was tossed away.

What could not be discarded was added to the mire and mass of unusable rubbish.

With the exponential increase in the population, refuse increased while space for disposal decreased, sometimes dramatically. Space was at a premium. From shelter to fresh water, from clean oxygen to cool air – even the climate changed. Yet the masses kept procreating. Rise in populations – and the shrinkage in available resources combined at an alarming rate, and preachers began spouting biblical prophecies of the end of days. The Four Horsemen. The devil. All those who did not believe were doomed to eternal damnation.

As if their current situation was not damning enough!

Despite dire pronouncements, the people remained complacent. Laws were broken and new laws promulgated, to no avail. Like an advancing hurricane, with plenty of warnings and much denial, scarcity became the focus. Food and water no longer sufficed, and world governments united out of necessity. Toward the end, there was essentially a single governing body, but that seemed irrelevant to the misery experienced by all. In time, news reports dealt only with pleasant stories, no doubt written by once affluent moguls, all in a spirit to keep the masses calm.

It was futile. The masses remained calm by virtue of vittles laced with drugs. There was no other way. And when one died, his remains would be whisked away by robotic mechanisms hooked up to the buildings. Sanitation was prized. Mechanization had become the Hal of an old movie.

Until nothing meant anything more.

* * *

Mark remained at my side, blankly staring into space, still holding me. Dawn had broken through the rain clouds, and the soft rays of a shy sun reluctantly shone through. There was no rainbow. There was nothing.

"Mark?" I whispered. He did not answer. "Mark? What are you thinking?" He stared out, blankly. His hand felt heavy on my shoulder. I turned his face toward me.

But he just stared into the void.

* * *

There was a time when the earth brimmed with greenery, when dewdrops fed the lilting streams and flowers graced the landscape. It was a time of promise and renewal.

I was born to revel in her gifts; celebrate the sunshine, carouse amid her fruits. Others, too, enjoyed her garlands. But the tides came in, and one by one erased all traces …

…and then there were none.

About The Author

I am a child of the world. My international background has given me a perspective on other cultures, and the austerity of my childhood trained me to look for answers where they were unexpected. All my experiences have melded into my upbringing, and have shaped my love of reading and writing. I write about subjects that I love, from music to technology, from nutrition to trading options on the stock market. I have published six books of romantic poetry.

My schooling began in Israel, and continued in Paris, then in the United States. I graduated Florida International University with studies in psychology, statistics, international finance, languages, eventually earning my degree in psychology with honors. It was during my graduate classes in psychology that I fell in love with the exacting process of writing and editing academic papers. Much later, when blogging became popular, I took up this personal form of writing, and currently maintain about 13 blogs. I have written extensively as a ghostwriter, as well as under my own byline. You may contact me at yael@pro-wordsmith.net.

Made in the USA
Middletown, DE
17 August 2016